AT HOME IN
THE SHADOWS

At Home in the the Shadows

by

Gary McMahon

Black Shuck Books
www.BlackShuckBooks.co.uk

Text Found on a Defunct Webpage was originally
published online as 'Under Offer' (The Hub, 2008)
The Chair was originally published in *Black Static* 10 (2009)
The Table was originally published in *It Knows Where You
Live* (Gray Friar Press, 2011)

Cover design & internal layout © WHITEspace 2019

First published in the UK by Black Shuck Books, 2019

978-1-913038-15-1

Dedicated to Sean Hogan:
A brother in art who does the devil's business

Text Found on a Defunct Webpage

We are pleased to offer for sale this modernised detached Victorian property. A viewing is recommended in order to appreciate the accommodation, which is situated with access to Leeds, Bradford and Wakefield and amenities to include shops, schools, bus transport routes. The accommodation comprises wide gravel drive with parking for up to three vehicles, entrance hall, lounge, fitted dining kitchen, cellar, three bedrooms and a bathroom wc whilst externally there are gardens to the front and rear with views over open fields and countryside beyond over the Tong Valley. Offers invited for a quick sale. Viewings: strictly by appointment only.

Entrance Hall –Decorative steel-barred double-glazed entrance door, radiator, stairs to first floor with access to large renovated space under staircase which has been fitted out with wall hooks, ceiling hoist, and low flat work bench.

Lounge –*13' 1" x 12' 5" (3.99m x 3.78m)* measured into bay. Double glazed bay window to front, feature fireplace (bricked in), soundproofing to walls (this feature is typical throughout whole property), radiator, dancing pole situated on low circular stage, spotlighting, manacles.

Kitchen / Dining Room –*16' 1" x 10' 0" (4.9m x 3.05m)* inc. units. Double glazed shuttered window and metal door to rear, radiator, fitted hollow wall and base units with work surfaces and specialised drainage channels, feature flooring with drainage gulleys, stainless steel sink and drainer, heavy duty industrial grinder and mount, plumbing for washing machine and dishwasher, space for appliance, huge stove with four ring hob and spacious caged oven with extractor, padlocked storage cupboard, spotlighting.

Cellar – *13' 1" x 12' 5" (3.99m x 3.78m)* Two-foot thick concrete walls, area sub-divided into four separate cramped cells with central walkway, water barrel with leather harness fixed above, bespoke wooden chair installation (wired to independent electricity supply), central stone well with concrete lid and no access ladder, stand-alone generator.

Stairs To:

First Floor Landing – Loft access, metal hatch; loft fitted out with various fetish apparatus and containing several impenetrable hardwood boxes with external locking mechanisms.

Master Bedroom – *11' 3" x 10' 0" (3.43m x 3.05m)* Double glazed barred window with heavy-duty shutters to front, radiator, mirrors affixed to ceiling, hatch in floor with access to cramped crawlspace beneath, large sliding compartment stowed under bed, lined with razorblades.

Bedroom – *10' 0" x 9' 0" (3.05m x 2.74m)* Double glazed barred window to rear, radiator, chains, light scratching to walls, comprehensive staining to wooden floor.

Bedroom – *8' 2" x 6' 0" (2.49m x 1.83m)* Double glazed barred window to front, radiator, small second window bricked over.

Bathroom – *6' 0" x 5' 8" (1.83m x 1.73m)* Black suite comprises wc, wash basin, bidet (with razored fittings), bath (slight red staining to interior) with shower (plumbed to offer scalding water only), radiator, spotlighting, double glazed barred window to rear.

Outside

Front Garden – Concrete laid over lawn, concrete bin filled with quicklime.

Rear Garden – Laid to lawn, with several ornamental stone markers, and has views over open fields, thick dark, dark woods and mile upon mile of open countryside beyond.

The
Chair

Ben found the long winter evenings hardest of all. When daylight ended early and the darkness that took its place was as hard and flat as sheet metal, he waited in vain for his father's shadow to arrive and cross the threshold into the house.

He waited for so long and he waited so often that it became habit, a ritual like so many others that made up the fabric of his near-monastic existence.

Sitting forlornly at the living room window, he watched the street, wishing that his father's car would appear, slowing as it approached the house to turn into the empty drive and park there.

His mother was usually busying herself in the kitchen – plating up a sparse meal for tomorrow, preparing his medication, or mixing herself a cocktail – and Ben's shoulders tensed at every sound she made, as if expecting a sudden stab of pain. The laboured twist of a lid. The eager chink of a glass. The deep sighs which bled from her willowy frame as she sat down heavily at the table to drink.

The street, however, remained empty and silent but for the occasional lone figure passing beneath the cold glare of streetlamps or a huddled group of strangers returning home from the pub, heads held close together as they whispered about things Ben would never know. None of these passers-by made much noise; they simply went on their way, leaving the street and its inhabitants unmolested.

One night at the start of December, just as the temperature was beginning to drop sharply towards full winter, Ben sat at his usual place by the window, chin resting on his fists, knees tucked up under his body as he waited for something to happen. He seemed to spend more than half his life waiting.

"Would you like a drink?" His mother's voice was slurred – it always was by this time of the day. Her evening cocktails had become more frequent, and stronger; he rarely saw her without a glass in her hand.

"No thanks." He continued to watch the street, scanning it for clues to something he would only know when he saw it. Or felt it.

"A sandwich, maybe? Or a bowl of that cereal you like so much?"

Ben shook his head, aware that his mother couldn't see his response but realising that one was not really needed.

He joined her in the lounge and they watched a gameshow where screaming contestants – each more overweight than the last – tried to guess the retail prices of electrical appliances, and then it was time for bed. Ben kissed her cheek, drawing back as soon as his lips touched her wet, rubbery skin, and then he headed for the door. He couldn't recall the last time his mother had tucked him in, although he knew she always entered his room before she retired to her own bed. She usually stood for a few minutes at the bottom of his bed, weeping, while Ben fought hard to convince her that he was sleeping. He could not guess what her reaction might be if she knew that he was awake.

"Don't forget to take your tablets." His mother spoke without taking her eyes from the television screen; they reflected a capering man in a grey suit, a drab audience perched on the edge of hysteria.

Ben took the small plastic cup from the mantelpiece and swallowed the three white pills dry, wondering what might happen if he ever forgot about them. Wishing that he had the courage to find out.

Upstairs, after brushing his teeth and emptying his bladder, Ben sat at his desk, staring at the sky beyond the streaky window. Big dark clouds shuffled across the vast grey expanse, seeming to rise and fall as they travelled across the horizontal. Faces appeared within them, eyes and noses and gaping mouths... the disinterested gods of his empty childhood.

Standing, Ben leaned upwards to open the window and let in a sharp breeze – the air inside the room was thick and heavy, as if it were carrying elements of his sorrow. As he pushed the latch into its socket, jamming the window open an inch and feeling the cold air brush against his cheek, he glanced down and saw the chair. It was perched outside a house a few doors along the street, positioned on the footpath directly in front of the gate of the property. It was an old dining chair: wooden back and legs, a beige plastic-coated cushion on its seat. The cushion looked worn, faded; its shape lumpy and distorted.

Ben was puzzled. Why would someone place a dining chair out there, right in the front street? If it had been left out for disposal by the bin men, it was a few days early (bin day wasn't until Friday and today was only Tuesday). He supposed the sight of the solitary chair might not be so strange during the summer, when it was conceivable that someone might have left it out after spending an afternoon lounging in the sun. But it was winter, and it was cold – the coldest he could remember in his short life. The weather reports were all predicting heavy snowfall by the end of the week, and a few dusty white flakes had even begun to fall earlier that evening.

No, the chair was a mystery, an oddity: something to distract his thoughts. What made it even more peculiar was the fact that Ben could not shake the feeling that he'd just missed seeing someone sitting in the chair; if he had been quicker, he might have witnessed that someone standing up and walking away. The feeling was frightening, yet it also made him feel alive.

The chair was gone when he got out of bed next morning. He'd dreamed of it, imagining a tall, straight-backed figure sitting there all through the night, so it was fresh in his mind when he woke. He almost ran to the window, and the sight of the empty spot on the footpath provoked a dull ache of disappointment in his stomach.

Ben turned away from the window and went downstairs, where he prepared his own breakfast. The plastic cup had been replaced on the mantelpiece – its rightful place, where both Ben and his mother would always see it – and three new pills sat at the bottom. He picked up the cup, poured the pills into his hand, and then walked back into the kitchen. He dropped the pills into the sink and turned on the cold tap. It took a long time for them to swirl down the plughole.

"Wow," he said, taken aback by his small act of rebellion. He tried to come up with a reason for not taking the pills, but none would come. He simply felt like missing a dose.

His mother emerged from her room as he was eating Rice Krispies. He heard her heavy footfalls above him, moving slowly across the landing. The bathroom door slammed shut. By the time his bowl was empty the toilet was being flushed. The sound was too loud, as if there was something wrong with the plumbing; pipes banged on the walls, like tiny fists demanding release from an unseen prison.

As his mother's footsteps creaked down the stairs, Ben choked back the urge to scream. Had the missed medication upset the delicate balance of his nerves? Surely, he thought, any side effects would take much longer to surface.

"Did you sleep okay?" His mother's eyes were barely open; her face slack, like an empty bag. She'd neglected to comb her hair and her dressing gown was buttoned up all wrong. "Did you get your breakfast?"

"I always do," said Ben, but the words missed their target, and she simply turned away to make a cup of tea.

Later that day it began to hail. The sky darkened, and splits opened within it, letting loose a mixture of rain and ice that sounded like gunshots against the window panes. Ben sat on the sofa and watched in awe: he'd always loved these extremes of weather. Rain, snow, hail...

these things excited him in a way that he failed to comprehend but enjoyed anyway.

His mother stayed in the kitchen for a long time, sitting at the dining table and nursing a bottle. Ben entered the room several times that morning, but his mother never moved. She stared at the same spot on the wall for hours, her eyes like stones pushed into the damp unmoving mask of her face.

The telephone rang at some point between noon and one o'clock. Ben stirred from his place at the window and picked up the receiver. The storm outside sounded loudly in his ear – too loud to properly make out the voice that was straining to be heard.

"Hello?"

"—couldn't do it. Not coming... going away—"

"Hello? Who is this?" The line was breaking up, swallowed by static. "Dad?"

The voice went quiet as soon as Ben said the word. The static cleared, but whoever was trying to speak suddenly clammed up, as if reluctant to reveal himself. The moment stretched past its breaking point. Ben glanced at the clock on the wall but for some reason couldn't seem to fathom the time.

"Is that you, Dad?"

The static swelled one final time, then broke apart, leaving behind a gap into which a voice stumbled: "I'm sorry, son. You must believe me. I never wanted any of this to happen – it wasn't what I planned. Just remember that I love you and I'll see you again... just not now. Not yet."

Was his father crying? Was that why the voice sounded so strained, so unlike the one he'd heard all his life, gently encouraging him from the background, urging him to be better, to face the things that he feared? "Dad?"

The line went dead. Ben replaced the receiver, surprised at how steady his hands were. Missing his medication that morning seemed like a blessing – usually, after such an awkward moment of social interaction, his hands would be twitching like frightened rabbits. He smiled, but the expression felt wrong on his face, like a wet rag pressed against his lips.

"Who-was-that?" His mother could barely construct a sentence: it came out as a single word.

"No one," said Ben, satisfied that he was still able to lie to her, to make her believe that he was doing okay and that everything would turn out fine, in time, after the remains of battle had been tidied away.

They did not speak again for the remainder of that day.

That night, the chair was outside again.

Ben went to bed early just to check, and it sat in the same place outside the same gate, on the same part of the footpath. He once again had the sense that the chair had been recently occupied – very recently; as if, in fact, whoever had been sitting there had got up and left the exact moment before Ben looked in its direction.

On closer inspection he could see that the chair's cushion was badly damaged. A split indentation marred its otherwise unbroken surface, as if a body too heavy had sat there for far too long. Ben tried to remember who lived there, in the house where the chair had appeared, but couldn't recall any overweight resident. In fact, he was sure that he'd never seen anyone coming or going from the property, apart from a small old lady who only ever seemed to potter around in the garden, pruning the bushes and digging in the wide soil borders.

He pressed his forehead against the window pane, trying to get closer to the chair without leaving the house. He hadn't left the house for several months – he wasn't sure quite how many; certainly almost as long as his father's absence, which had begun immediately after the final argument between his parents. To go outside now would take an act of will that his medication was designed to smother.

Was that why he'd chosen to miss his pills? He'd done the same this evening, before climbing the stairs – holding them in the side of his cheek until he could reach the bathroom to flush them away. He'd watched as they swirled in the pan, little white pellets caught up in a storm.

Ben's eyes ached but he couldn't blink. He was afraid that if he moved his gaze from the chair for even a split second, he might miss catching sight of its owner. For some reason, the thought of this filled him with a horror that felt bigger than the house, even larger than the sky above it: a gargantuan terror that could never be allowed out into the open.

He sat at the window until his eyelids grew too heavy to support and his body began to slump. Tiredness dragged him towards his bed, and he was sleeping even before he fell lifelessly onto the soft mattress.

His mother failed to rise the following morning. All during breakfast he waited for the sounds of her stirring, but by 11 a.m. she still had not shifted. He imagined her dead up there, lying flat and stiff having choked on her tongue during the night; or perhaps she'd suffered a sudden heart attack in her sleep. He put it off for as long as he could, but by the time morning TV became afternoon TV he knew that he must investigate.

Ben climbed the stairs with feet heavy as his conscience. He crossed the landing and stood outside his mother's bedroom door, hands hanging limp by his sides, feet pointed slightly inwards. After what seemed like hours, he finally reached out to open the door. His sweaty hand clenched the handle and he pushed, flinching as the door's bottom edge scraped with a sound like claws across the too-thick carpet.

"Mum?"

There was no answer. The room was dark and silent; not even a chink of light was visible through the closed curtains. His mother hated the daylight – she was a light sleeper, and even the slightest hint of illumination in the room would wake her. She'd bought special blackout curtains to hang at the windows, and the darkness they produced was as thick as tar and just as hard to penetrate.

"Mother?" That was better: the more formal address felt more comfortable in his mouth.

Ben crept forward, aware that his feet did not want to move, but forcing them on anyway, knowing that if he did not look now, he would never feel strong enough to enter this room again. He kicked something in the darkness, a small hard item; bottles clinked joylessly at his feet.

"Time to get up... it's past lunch time."

By now he was certain that the room was empty – it felt empty, smelled empty, even sounded empty in the way that his voice died as soon as it left his lips. As his hand fell onto the pillows lined up along the top of his mother's bed, propped haphazardly against the quilted headboard, he fully expected to feel no head resting upon them, no hair sprayed out across the soft material... he stared down at his hands as they clutched one of the pillows, not quite understanding when or why he had picked it up.

His fists clenched inside the puffy mass, fingers straining to meet. The joints of his fingers and wrists felt sore.

"Mother." It was not a question, nor was it a request; not even a cry for help. It was a word, just a word; one that meant less every time he said it. He put the pillow back on the bed and took a step backwards, as if denying something he was barely able to grasp.

Slowly, he turned away and left the room, closing the door firmly behind him.

Ben ate a late lunch that day. There wasn't much in the fridge, so he did the best he could with what he found in the cupboards – a few slices of bread, some stale cheese, half a jar of pickled onions. Not once did it cross his mind to call anyone, the police or other authorities: the absence of his mother was not a problem, nor did it seem like something he should expend much energy worrying about.

He washed the dishes and put away the plate and cutlery he'd used during his meal. His hands were as steady as wooden boards; he wasn't missing his medication at all. Had his mother been forcing him to take it so she could manage him better? If that were the case, he was glad she had vanished. It was unfair for her to attempt to manipulate his emotions in such a way.

"I'm all alone now," he said, and the words tasted good: sweet and somehow bitter on his tongue. But the bitterness was not unpleasant, it was strangely rewarding in a way that the chalky little pills could never be. "*Aaaaaaallllllll* alone. He giggled and jerked in shock at the sound and shape of his own voice as it wormed around and into the folds of his ears.

Ben watched the shows on television that his mother never allowed – cop shows and comedies she deemed unsuitable for his nervous disposition. The sound of his own laughter was like a balm; the feelings he was now experiencing made him tingle all over.

Voices passed by outside the window, but they spoke no language Ben could recognise. He listened to the alien words, the garbled phrases, until they were well out of earshot.

Time passed. He stayed up late and ate the rest of the food he found in the cupboard. Despite the staleness of the produce he discovered there, he had rarely tasted such intense flavours. The cheese was stronger than a slap in the face, the biscuits melted on his tongue, the baked beans were like angels' eggs bursting against his teeth. Even water from the tap sent tiny explosions of excitement along his throat.

He climbed the stairs to bed long after midnight, relishing the fact that he'd stayed up past his usual allotted bedtime. Everything felt different at this hour – even the strange pelt of the carpet beneath his feet was like nothing he'd ever known before. His hands skimmed against the brittle walls, taking pleasure from the raised pattern of the wallpaper, a vivid design he'd not noticed until now.

When he went to the toilet it felt as if he were crapping a rainbow.

Once in his room, stationed like a sniper at the window, he stared at the old dining chair along the street. It was in the same spot it had occupied the previous two nights, but this time something was different. Tonight, instead of retaining the rumour of a recent presence, the chair was occupied.

His mother sat motionless in her creased nightdress, spine held stiff and straight against the wooden back of the chair, as if held suspended in either the dull spotlight of the moon or the unflinching gaze of a streetlight. A mute performer upon a strange stage, awaiting direction; her hands were clasped, unmoving, in her narrow lap, and her arms were pressed tightly against the sides of her rigid body. She did not move. Even her feet remained flat on the ground, as if glued or nailed in place. The exposed skin of her forearms and legs was stippled with what looked like henna tattoos – thin black lines and splashes that traced the hidden routes of her veins.

If he allowed himself, Ben could imagine that she was stuck there, lashed into a strict sitting position by invisible ropes; but he did not want to think such troubling thoughts. Instead, he simply watched his mother's terrible baggy face, peered into the bottomless holes of her eyes, and watched her weep black tears for something held just out of reach – possibly by Ben's father, or perhaps, he suddenly understood, even by Ben himself.

Quietly, patiently, Ben sat at the window, waiting to see what would happen when, finally, she tried to stand. Wondering if his father might walk along the street and join her, clasping her hand as they strode towards the house to fetch him.

The
Table

It was there when he got home, standing at the front of the lounge, wedged into the belly of the bay window. Ben noticed it immediately – he would do, of course, because when he left the house to go to work that morning, he didn't own a dining table; and now, here one was, where before there had been nothing but bare carpet.

He put his wallet and keys on the top shelf of the bookcase, as usual, and walked across the room, never taking his eyes off the new piece of furniture. It was an ordinary pine table, a bit worn at the edges but in reasonably good condition. Like something you might pick up cheap in a second-hand shop. Someone had varnished the wood, and it shone in the gloom. The surface was pitted here and there with tiny marks and scratches, and if he looked hard enough and allowed his mind to form patterns, some of them began to look like they might have been intended to represent numbers or letters.

Ben reached out and turned on the main light; the marks on the tabletop faded beneath the intense illumination. The varnish shone.

As tables went, it was nice enough, but he had no idea what it was doing there.

He went to the phone and lifted the receiver, dialled Jill's number. The phone rang eight times before she picked it up.

"It's me," he said, staring at a spot on the wall where the paint was fading. He'd have to do something about that eventually.

"Hi. How... are you okay?"

"Yeah. Fine."

"Listen. About last night. We should talk."

"Forget about it. We were both drunk." He twirled the phone cord in his fingers, thinking that he might replace the item with a cordless model. He didn't have a mobile; there was no need for him to embrace that technology, whatever Jill said. "I have something else I want to say."

"But we should talk. Really talk."

"A table."

Jill went silent.

"A table," he said again.

"What the fuck are you talking about, Ben? What's this with the table?"

"That's what I'm asking you. What's with the table? I know you said I needed some new furniture, but if you wanted to get me some, I think a chair or a sofa might have been a more appropriate gift."

"You're evading the issue again. Why won't you talk to me?"

"How did you even get it in here? I never gave you a key."

"Quit it with the table talk, Ben. I believe in us."

"Did one of the lads help you? I gave Maccas a spare key. It was him, wasn't it?"

"Talk to me, Ben. We can't go on like this."

"I don't know what you mean. Listen, I'll speak to you later. I have a headache." He put down the phone. Jill was still talking, but her words were beginning to sound like bad song lyrics. *I believe in us.* Just what the hell was that supposed to mean anyway?

He looked again at the table, at its delicate knotty surface, at the half-visible scratches in the wood. It was darker nearer the centre, perhaps where something had been spilled. He wondered if it would clean up nice, or if the stain was permanent. There were no matching chairs; just the table. It looked odd that way, somehow impermanent.

Later that evening, after eating a microwave meal and sipping a can of tepid lager, Ben sat in the dark fast-forwarding through a DVD. He was restless, couldn't settle. Light from the television played across the carpet at his feet, creeping steadily towards him. He lifted his feet up onto the chair, tucking them beneath his bottom. Glancing out of the window and into the small back garden, he watched the bushes sway like drunken line-dancers in the wind.

Bored, he pressed pause on the DVD remote control. On the screen, a Japanese warrior ceased mid-swing with his sword, cutting the air. Ben glanced to his left, towards the dark bay window, and saw that someone was sitting at the table. There were four of them, gathered around as if waiting for a meal. They all stared across the top of the table – not really at each other, just into the air above the middle of the table, where the darkness seemed somehow pinched or folded.

Ben didn't feel afraid. He stared at them: a man, a woman, two children – a boy and a girl. They all had dark hair, pale faces: they looked vaguely oriental. He couldn't make out much more regarding their features because of the darkness and the fact that their faces looked smudged, like paints running together. None of the people moved; they all stared at the same point above the centre of the table.

The air was still. Ben couldn't even hear his own breathing. He was afraid to look away from the family – yes, that was it. They were a family. He stared at them for what felt like a long time but was probably only the space of a few minutes. He didn't blink. Then, finally, he was able to tear his gaze away from the group. He glanced at the door that led out to the hall, at the silent warrior on the TV screen, and when he looked back at the table they were gone. Gone, but still there, under the surface – he could still make out the way the darkness clung to them, like old sheets.

Ben turned off the television, got out of the chair, and climbed the stairs to bed. Even though he could no longer see them he knew that the four figures were still there, sitting silently at the table, and the thought comforted him. He thought about them as he drifted off to sleep and was puzzled to realise that he couldn't recall the specifics of what they looked like.

He dreamt of his mother, sitting in an old dining chair at the roadside – perhaps a chair that had once belonged with the table in his lounge. The street was empty; the houses were all derelict. There were black marks on his mother's skin, thick scrawls and curlicues across her face and arms. Her eyes were open. She was crying, but silently. After a while he realised that she was tied to the chair and unable – rather than unwilling – to move.

The next day he rang around his friends and asked each of them if they had helped Jill with the table. None of them knew anything about it – or that was what they claimed. The whole thing was a mystery. He began to doubt that Jill had arranged delivery of the table; it was as if it had simply appeared in his house, perhaps summoned by some obscure need.

Just before lunch, when he was thinking about going out for a pint and a toasted sandwich at his local, the doorbell rang. Ben put down the book he'd been reading – Dostoevsky's *The Idiot*, because he was trying to catch up with the classics – and went to answer the door.

Jill was standing on the step, her hair mussed by the wind, faint spatters of drizzle on her face and shoulders. She was trying to smile but couldn't quite master the technique; her mouth looked twisted, as if she were suffering from the effects of a mild stroke. "Hi. I thought you might like some company."

Ben stepped aside. "Okay. I was just thinking about lunch – fancy some cheese on toast?" He walked backwards, into the hall, and motioned her inside. Jill followed him, shrugging off her coat, and as she stepped over the threshold dark clouds moved across the sun and abruptly it began to rain.

She stood behind him in the kitchen as he prepared the toast, laying thick slices of cheddar across the buttered surface and returning them to the grill. He boiled the kettle and made instant coffee; the room smelled of burning. Rain hammered at the windows, shutting them in. The air grew warm and heavy.

"We still need to talk," said Jill as he passed her a plate. She had taken off her shoes, and her bare soles whispered on the vinyl floor as she shifted her weight from foot to foot. "We can't keep fighting like we did the other night – we won't last two minutes if we can't stop getting at each other's throats."

He stared at her neck, at the pale, loose flesh. She was getting old; the skin there was starting to tighten. "I know," he said. "I'm sorry. I feel... detached lately, like I'm not really here. I shouldn't take it out on you." He heard the words but didn't feel them; they were less than meaningless.

She followed him into the lounge. "Is that the famous table?" Crumbs scattered across her chin as she bit into her toast. She cocked her head, indicating the bay window.

"Yeah. Are you sure you didn't buy it?"

"I think I'd remember if I had. And besides, why the hell would I buy you a table... and a second-hand one at that?" The rain did its best to drown out her words, but he could still hear them. She licked her lips; her eyes glistened in the half-light.

They finished eating and sipped their coffee. Ben thought it tasted bitter, but Jill didn't mention what she thought. She watched him closely, carefully, throughout the meal, as if waiting for the right moment to strike.

They kissed because he thought they should; it was perfunctory, an act lacking in real passion. Jill tried to push him to the floor, but he shook his head and drew her across the room, tugging her by the hand towards the bay window, and the table. She leaned back across the tabletop, bringing up her legs and wrapping them around his waist. He felt cold; her skin was like ice. She could not touch him inside, where it counted.

He pushed her across the polished surface, forcing his pelvis between her legs. Her skirt rode up around her thighs and he pawed at her breasts. She clawed at his buttocks. They went on like this for a while, and then Ben pulled away, stepping back from her. He thought she looked like a sacrificial offering, spread-eagled there on the table, with her top buttons undone and her skirt in disarray. She was panting hard; sweat shone on her chest and forehead. Ben thought that he heard a snatch of music, just for a second, but then it was gone. Perhaps someone had walked by the window with music playing on their mobile phone, or a car had gone by with the windows open and the stereo turned up loud.

The four figures were sat once again at the table, each in the same place as before. There were no chairs – they hovered above the floor, as if seated, and held their arms out across the table, palms upward. Jill's head was resting at the centre of the table, right at the point where their sightlines converged. A crimped halo of darkness hung directly above her. She was looking at him, her eyes reflecting a kind of pleading; clearly, she could not see the family.

"I can't," he said, not quite knowing what he meant but realising that the family would understand even if he didn't. Their faces were immobile, lacking real expressions, yet he had the sense that beneath their skin they were struggling to express some inner emotion – the muscles beneath their blurred faces tensed, twitching as if insects had burrowed into their cheeks. Something was on the verge of breaking through; he could feel it; he could taste it, like electricity on the tongue.

Jill stood and rearranged her clothes in silence. She glared at him as she stalked across the room. In the hall, she pulled on her coat and opened the door. Then she paused, as if waiting for him to approach her, to perhaps beg her to stay. Ben remained where he was; the family sat at the table. Jill slammed the door behind her. He watched her through the bay window as she was slowly erased by the rainfall. He knew that he would never see her again.

The table was empty once again, but they were there; they were always there, waiting for a meal that never came, a form of sustenance that was constantly denied them.

Miraculously, Ben managed to get an appointment with the doctor early the next day – someone had cancelled, and the slot was free if he was prepared to go down to the surgery immediately. He went out into the light rain, running beneath a sullen sky. The surgery was not far from his house, and a short cut took him through a series of identical wet streets and right to the door.

He must be ill: that would explain everything. A reoccurrence of the depressive fits and mood-swings from his childhood.

The doctor was sceptical when Ben told her about his experience with the table.

"I read your file," she said, smiling blandly. "I know you have a history of mental issues, and that your mother was a severe depressive. You know that it's all about mood management, don't you? In your case, you're the best person to do this. I could prescribe you all kinds of pills, but I'd rather use that as a last resort. I don't want to put you through all that again unless I have to."

She typed notes into a computer keyboard as she spoke. It didn't fill Ben with confidence.

"I don't want medication," said Ben, wishing that he had never come here. "I just want you to tell me that I'm not mad, that everything's okay." His hands twitched in his lap; he moved his feet on the carpet in tiny circles. "Tell me I'm not slipping away again, like before. Like my mother."

"You're not mad. You just need to manage your condition. What happened when you were younger – your parents, particularly your mother's disappearance – left scars. It was bound to. Maybe counselling would help? Someone to talk to? I can give you a couple of numbers to try, but be aware that the waiting lists are long."

He took the information the doctor offered –
three printed sheets – and left the surgery,
wishing that he had stayed at home.

Ben didn't want someone to talk to. He knew
that the people at the table were not imaginary
representations of his own absent family – that
would have been much too simple. His father
had left when he was young, and his mother had
disappeared during Ben's long illness. The
police had searched everywhere for her, but she
had never been found.

Even now, he didn't miss her; not really. He
missed the idea of a mother more than the
physical reality. She had been depressed, yet her
doctor had failed to recognise the signs. Ben, in
his misguided attempts to make her love him,
had become ill by proxy and allowed the woman
to smother him.

It was a period in his life that he chose not to
discuss. Even Jill knew little about his teenage
years. It was better that way; there were no
awkward questions, no issues to dodge.

There was something bigger going on here
than his petty problems. The family might be
taken for ghosts, but again that idea was too
simple-minded. They were something different

– something more forlorn and complicated. They were more like the ghosts of ghosts.

When they appeared at the table, it was as if he was being allowed a glimpse into another place; somehow the table linked them to the world, or perhaps it trapped them here, momentarily, so that he might see them. He wondered if, in that other place, they sat down at a table that became the one in his lounge, or if they were bound to it, imprisoned in an otherwise bare chamber to participate in a kind of enforced mediumship...

But these were useless thoughts. Like all enigmas, the beauty of this one lay in the fact that it could never be unravelled. There was a table, and sometimes four people sat around it, without chairs. That was all.

Later that evening he went through his address book and looked at the names of old girlfriends. Not one of them had reached him enough to make him want to start his own family. Even Jill, despite being the best of them all, he had kept at a distance. Was there a failing in him, or was it something about these women that doomed all his relationships to end the same way? He couldn't remember his father,

and his mother's face remained out of reach...
none of the women he had ever lain with had
been able to replace these dim memories with
new ones.

He took a long bath and read a chapter from
his book. When he returned to the lounge they
were there again, sitting in their usual places
around the table. The children looked to be aged
between eight and ten; the parents were possibly
in their mid-thirties. Once again, their faces
were rigid and indistinct, but seemed just about
to move. Ben felt that whenever he looked away
from them, they were pulling faces at him, and
when he looked back their faces were once again
expressionless.

"Who are you?" He did not expect an answer
and wasn't surprised when none came. "Please,
tell me. Who are you? Why are you here?" There
was no reason; they simply were.

"When I was a boy, I used to long for a family
like this, sitting around a table at meal times. It's
something I never had." He approached the
table and stared at its centre, following their
gaze. The air there seemed to boil, rippling and
undulating as if something were trying to take
shape. He watched in silence, willing it to form,

but the sequence never reached its conclusion and the changes that threatened to occur never did. There was just that same rippling movement; a slow churning clot of thickened air above the stained area of tabletop.

On impulse Ben took off his shoes and climbed up onto the table, his knees aching and his stocking feet slipping slightly as he hauled himself up there. He stood within that knot of shifting air, feeling nothing as it wrapped around his midriff. The family stared at him, the skin of their faces pulled taut. Their eyes were huge, straining to see something that was never quite there.

Ben closed his eyes and threw back his head, waiting for something to change. When he opened his eyes, he was alone, standing on a table in the darkness. He felt foolish, as if he'd been tricked. He climbed down and crossed the room, where he sat in his solitary armchair and stared at the wall, not even recognising his own thoughts.

It seemed like hours later when the telephone rang. The curtains were open; the darkness outside pressed against the windows. He went to the telephone and picked it up. "Hello?"

"I rang to tell you that it's over." It took him a second or two to realise that the voice on the line belonged to Jill. At first, he'd thought it was his mother, calling from out of the past.

He didn't know what she wanted him to say.

"I thought I owed you at least the decency of telling you that I never want to see you again. I thought you might ask me to change my mind..."

He shook his head, unable to summon the words to tell her how he felt – unable to even understand how he felt.

"So that's it, then? You're happy that it's over?"

"Jill."

"Yes?" If there was hope in her voice, he was no longer able to recognise it.

"The table."

"Fuck the table, Ben. Fuck the fucking table... and fuck you, too." It was a memorable line on which to end a relationship; he was glad that he was able to give her that at least. She could tell her friends about it later, in the pub, when the pain went away.

Ben returned to his chair. He grabbed it and dragged it round so that it faced the bay window, and the table. Then he sat down and waited. He waited for a long time, but it was no time at all, not really, in the scheme of things. He sensed that others, elsewhere, had waited a lot longer, and for a lot less.

They appeared between blinks; interstitial apparitions, locked between moments. The man, the woman and the two children. They were the same, yet they were different. Something about them had changed, but Ben could not discern exactly what it was. Perhaps it was he who had changed, released now from the last thing binding him to this life.

He stood and walked across the room, stepped up onto the table. This time it was easier. His knees didn't ache, his mind was clear. He sat down on the table and crossed his legs, closing his eyes against the darkness. He felt them watching him – or rather, they stared at the dense space he occupied above the centre of the table. The stirring air pushed against his chest. This time he felt it, and the sensation was both terrifying and strangely comforting, like the uninvited caress of a stranger.

A sense of complete dislocation overcame him, casting him adrift from himself, and a buzzing sound filled his ears. It sounded like hundreds of bees, or strange droning music. A moment later Ben realised that he was crying. His cheeks were wet, his eyes were dripping.

Moist eyes. Wet hands.

He opened his eyes and stared at his cupped palms: they were filled with blood. He glanced at the man, the woman, and the children; at their blurred faces and their staring eyes. They were watching him now – he had their full attention at last.

They smiled in unison, the skin of their faces finally preparing to change or fall away to expose their true features beneath.

Ben reached out with his red hands and was not at all surprised when he felt them clasped by other hands. Small fingers wrapped around his wrists, pinning him to the table. He stared at the man. At the woman. At the children. He smiled as their thin skin peeled back to reveal what had always been there, just waiting for him to open his eyes and see them.

He thought of his missing mother and his absent father, of his loveless life and his heavy, heavy heart. Then, calmly, he accepted the kinship of the twitching crimson things which even now were rising from the table and moving slowly forward to embrace him.

On the Walls

Jill had driven the two-hundred miles to her mother's house many times before, but each of those journeys had ended with her mother being there, usually ready to brew a pot of tea and talk about things that meant a lot to her but nothing to Jill. Sometimes she talked about things that meant nothing to either of them – she just talked, filling the space between them with her words.

This time, however, her mother was not waiting. This time, nobody was waiting. Just the old house and the memories it held within its walls.

She pulled over at a motorway service station twenty-odd miles from her destination, just to take stock; to have a little break and drink some hot coffee. It was getting late. Nobody on the roads but the lost and the lonely, and those poor bastards who drove for a living.

After ordering an Americano from a tired-looking barista, she sat at a table by the window, doodling with a ballpoint pen on a paper napkin. Beyond the service station restaurant's oasis of light, the darkness was punctuated by tall sodium lights; pools of illumination gathered like bright puddles. Night pressed against the glass. She sipped her too-hot coffee and thought about her mother.

Jill felt that she had not yet grieved properly. It was two months since the woman's death, and she had not once shed a tear. Searching inside herself for a reaction, she found only a small, cramped space where her emotions should be.

She drank more coffee. It was cooler now, so she could at least take a mouthful. Outside, in the car park, a small girl walked into the light. She was dressed in a floral dress, sandals, knee-high socks.

Jill put down her cup. She stared at the girl, wondering who would let a child wander around alone this late at night – and why was she awake anyway? She should be in bed, cuddling a teddy bear, or curled up in the duvet bathed in an iPad's deathly glow.

Still staring, she began to stand.

A woman emerged from behind a parked lorry, took the girl's hand, and bent at the waist to speak to her, mouth to ear. The girl smiled, held out her arms. The woman picked her up and held her close, smiling as the girl kicked her feet in excitement.

Holding hands, they hurried to a waiting car. Through the dirt-smeared windscreen, the man at the wheel looked solemn and dangerous; but as soon as he caught sight of the woman and the girl, a smile transformed his face into something beautiful.

Jill looked away, something inside her clenching. Or perhaps unclenching.

Still on her feet, she gulped down her coffee and left the building, walking slowly to her car. Only now did she feel like crying, but she had no idea why, or for whom.

Back on the motorway, she took solace in the generic tunes played on a local radio station and the banal chatter of the absurdly cheery deejay. The remaining miles were eaten up in this way. She looked at the road, at the rear-view mirror, and wondered if this was all there would ever be. Her and the road; her and some endless journey without a real destination; her either running away from or falling towards something undefined.

When the slipway came up, she almost missed it, signalling at the last minute and swerving into the correct lane. Someone who was too far behind her to be in any real danger sounded their horn. She raised her hand, the middle finger extended and facing towards the car's rear window, and then slowed down as she approached the junction.

Three more miles and she would be there. She knew these minor roads intimately, as if they were an extension of the arteries in her body. Life had once flowed along these passageways, but now there was only the cold and the dark and the promise of nothing she had ever wanted.

When she pulled up outside her mother's house, she sat in the car with the engine running. The windows were dark; the building looked hostile. Her phone was charging in the dashboard socket. She picked it up and scanned through her messages. There was nothing important, only another text from David.

"Hello, Mum." Her voice sounded small inside the car. "I've come home again."

A man walking a small dog glanced her way as he crossed the road in front of the car. He was wearing a flat cap and a long overcoat, wrapped up against the chill. She smiled. He nodded. The dog jumped up at his legs as he paused in his stride. Then he walked away, dismissing her.

Unable to put it off any longer, Jill got out of the car and walked towards the house, her shoes sounding too loud on the concrete pavement in the quiet street. Stopping before the house, she looked up at it and wondered what the hell she'd been thinking of. She couldn't stay here, not tonight. Not ever again. It had been a foolish idea to even consider.

There was a hotel three miles away. She could stay there, just for the weekend, until she'd finished what needed to be done.

She turned away and went back to the car, the windows of the house watching her, unjudging, dispassionate. The house did not care how she felt; her lack of grief did not move it in any way.

It was just a house. Not even a home – not any longer.

The drive to the hotel didn't take long. The roads were quiet, the sky was dark, the moon bright. The girl at reception looked too young to be up this late, but she was efficient and found it easy to smile.

In her room, Jill unpacked and hung up her clothes in the narrow wardrobe. She changed her underwear and got into her sweat pants and T shirt. It was too late to have a shower: the spray of water would wake her up when all she wanted to do was sleep.

Her phone vibrated as she placed it on the nightstand. Checking it, she noted that she had three new messages, all from the same person. David.

Picking up the phone, she opened the messages. They all asked the same question: what time do you get here?

He was keen to see her, but she wasn't sure if she ever wanted to see him again. He was a part of her life that was behind her, a fragment from the past. If their brief affair had not quite been the biggest mistake of her life, it had certainly been an ill-advised tryst. David was married then, albeit in name only. He and his wife had not slept together in years. But he'd been married all the same.

Married meant complications. Hassle she didn't need in her life. It had been fun at first, but then he'd fallen for her and it had all turned to shit. He was too serious, too clingy; he wanted more of her than she was ever prepared to give. She was fresh out of another complex relationship, with a man who had left town without even saying goodbye after she'd ended it, so what she didn't need was more problems. Her old boyfriend had not been there enough; David had wanted to be there too much. Now that he was divorced, things could easily become even more complicated.

Deleting the messages, she lay back on the bed and let the phone drop onto the mattress. She closed her eyes and tried to picture her mother's face, but all she saw was the darkness. Soon it claimed her, and as she fell, the old woman's face finally appeared, surging towards her, eyes open, small, pinched mouth moving to form angry words that she could not hear, could never hear, because she didn't want to listen.

The sound of traffic on the road outside woke her before 6AM. She showered, dressed, and was out of the room in less than an hour. Forgoing the hotel breakfast, she ate a cereal bar from her bag – one of the small stashes she always carried with her, in case she wanted a low-fat snack. Jill worked hard to stay slim: four times a week at the gym, running and circuit training at the weekends. Her mother had been prone to fat; Jill was terrified of going the same way.

She parked in front of the house and walked up the path without pausing to think. Action, that was the trick: keep moving, keep working, don't start overthinking everything like she always did.

When she opened the door, it seemed as if the house exhaled. It was a silly idea, but that was the thought that crossed her mind in that moment.

It's breathing out...like a sigh.

She stepped inside and shut the door. Emptiness enveloped her, wrapping its cold arms around her body, holding her close. She put her bag on the telephone table at the bottom of the stairs and went through into the kitchen. Everything was still so clean and bright, as if her mother had only just cleaned the place. In her mind, she'd pictured dust and cobwebs, but the reality was much less grim.

She filled the kettle and set it to boil, grabbing the teabags from the cupboard where they had always been kept. Her mother would have been horrified that she wasn't making a proper pot of tea; it was a ritual, one of the many small rites that had kept her mother tethered to the world.

"Sorry, Mum. I can't be arsed." Her voice sounded tiny in the kitchen, an echo of her childhood rants. She smiled but didn't feel it. A leaden weight sat inside her.

She took down a mug from the shelf and popped a teabag inside. There was a crack in the mug, so she changed it. The second one was damaged too.

Everything's cracked. Every little thing is broken.

She swapped mugs again. This one was fine, apart from a tiny hairline crack near the handle, bisecting the head of a hand-painted daisy.

When the kettle had boiled, she made her tea and retreated to the living room. Her mother's furniture was modern. Despite her love of the past, she kept her decor up-to-date. Technology wasn't her favourite thing, so the television was a basic model rather than a Smart TV, and her one concession to the onslaught of the new had been to throw out her analogue radio and replace it with a digital model.

Jill sat on the sofa and slipped off her shoes. Stretching out her toes, she lay back and tried not to remember the good times she'd experienced in this house. It wasn't difficult; most of the times had been bad. When her father was alive, he'd been so quiet that they barely knew he was there. Her mother had been even more domineering back then – abusive, if she was honest. The woman had mentally and emotionally abused her husband for most of their marriage.

The only thing that kept them together was their daughter. She knew this; her father had told her once, when she'd found him sitting in the kitchen in the dark one night when she'd returned from a schoolfriend's house.

At the time, she'd been a typical teenager, embarrassed by her father's show of emotion. Two months later, when he passed away, she wished she'd done more than squeeze his thin, cold hand and say "G'night, Dad, you silly old fool."

She adjusted her position on the sofa, tucking her feet up under her thighs. Her eyes scanned the room, the walls. That horrible feature wall, with the flock wallpaper featuring black flowers against a yellow background. What had her mother been thinking when she bought that paper? It was disgusting.

Jill noticed that one of the joints had become separated, a small flap of paper folding downwards. She put her mug on the floor and crossed the room, reaching out to touch the paper. The flap came away in her hand, the paper pulling away from the wall. She wished the paper had come off the walls of her flat this easily, when she redecorated last year.

She pulled.

The sheet of paper came away without tearing, creating a larger flap that diagonally bisected that part of the wall. The plaster beneath was smooth but stained brown with age and ancient paste. There was a mark on the wall, as if something had been drawn there before the paper was applied.

A memory flashed across her mind: Jill, as a small child, using her crayons on the bare walls after they'd been stripped but before they were decorated.

"No way…"

She pulled again at the edge of the paper, using both hands to try and remove the entire sheet. It tore, but she managed to pick at it with her nails and gain another edge. She pulled again.

Within minutes, there was a small mound of torn wallpaper on the carpet and half of the wall was stripped bare.

The drawing she'd uncovered prompted no further memories. All she could recall was drawing flowers and a smiling sun. She had not drawn this; she was certain of it.

The drawing was of a monster. It had a large, spiny head with a single eye at the centre of its brow, a pig-like snout, and a mouth that took up more than just the bottom half of its face. The mouth was filled with jagged, uneven teeth. So many teeth that even this large a mouth could not contain them.

The monster was naked, but it possessed no indication of gender. Its arms were covered in scales; its legs were furred; its torso was transparent, so the internal organs could be viewed. No bones. Two hearts, one on each side of the chest, a stomach, some curly purple tubes that were clearly supposed to represent its guts.

The monster's right arm was hanging down by its side. The left arm was angled away from the body, the hand hidden beneath the next sheet of wallpaper. The visible hand was decorated with what looked like a flower of claws.

Shrugging, Jill started on the next sheet of wallpaper. This one didn't come away as easily, parts of it still sticking to the wall. She kept at it, picking, tearing, even rubbing with the palm of her hand when she needed to. Eventually, the rest of the paper came away from the wall.

The not-quite cartoon monster was holding the hand of another figure – a woman, judging by its flowery dress and long hair. The woman was holding the hand of a man. The man was holding the hand of a small girl who cowered near the corner of the room. The woman was either smiling broadly or screaming; the man had only rudimentary features; the girl was most definitely crying: there were big blue crayon tears spraying out of her oversized eyes.

Jill backed slowly away from the mural. She recognised the crude draughtsmanship as her own, when she'd been five or six years old, but the image meant nothing to her. She had no recollection of sketching the monster, and when she searched her mind all she could remember was drawing pretty things – sunshine, flowers, animals. As a child, she had never created such dark material as this.

Sitting down on the sofa, she stared at the grotesque scene. The childish drawing held a power that surprised her. Despite its primitive technique, there was a sense of horror, of helplessness that drove the image into her brain. Whoever had drawn this, they had intended it as a desperate cry for help.

Pushing thoughts of the picture from her mind, she stood and left the room. The stairwell felt more cramped than ever as she climbed the stairs to the first floor and her mother's room. Walking along the landing, she glanced at the pictures on the walls – bland landscapes, photos of places but none of people.

The door to her mother's room was shut. Jill stood outside on the landing, staring at the door handle. As she watched, detached from the moment, her hand grabbed it and turned. The door swung slowly open, and she stepped inside.

The room was neat and tidy. The old double bed took centre stage against the main wall. The tall triple wardrobe dominated the west side of the room. There was a dressing table and chair under the window, a small chest of drawers and a bedside cabinet. Her mother had never liked clutter, so there were no ornaments or unnecessary items lying around. Just the essentials.

Jill took the chair and placed it in front of the wardrobe, then stood on it to reach the cupboard doors at the top of the piece of furniture. Inside one of them, she found a big old cardboard box with the words "Papers and stuff" written on the side in thick black marker pen. This was where her mother kept all the insurance policies and important paperwork someone might need in the instance of her death. Her birth certificate, marriage license, the deeds to the house.

She climbed down, struggling a little, and put the box on the bed, sitting down next to it. The mattress creaked. Sunlight bled through the window, highlighting dust motes that spun slowly in the air like drunken insects. After a slight pause, she opened the box.

The top layers consisted of the kind of official paperwork she was here to retrieve, but underneath that she found something surprising. Her old sketchbooks, the ones she'd used as a child – at least some of them. Two thin A3 sized volumes, the pages filled with the drawings she used to love doing when she was small, and the world had seemed so large.

Lifting one of the sketchbooks out of the box, she flipped the pages. Among other things, it contained linework prototypes of the family she'd seen downstairs: crudely drawn representations of her mother, her father, and herself.

But no monsters.

She took the books, and the paperwork, and went back downstairs. She placed them inside the large bag-for-life she'd brought along to help her carry her findings out to the car.

Glancing at the living room door, she experienced a strange feeling that was part nostalgia, part terror. There was no name for the emotion; it was something that simply rose within her and then sank again, disappearing beneath the more identifiable emotions of guilt, sorrow, and grief.

The rest of the day was spent going through cupboards, drawers, box files; opening old cardboard boxes, stained brown envelopes, and dog-eared photo albums. There wasn't much left here; a lot of her mother's most treasured possessions had been either sold or given away once she'd learned that she was about to die. This stuff constituted the remnants. The things that had been ignored or forgotten. She stuffed anything useful into two smaller boxes and moved them to the boot of the car.

Before leaving the house, she went back into the living room to look once again at the drawing on the wall. Staring at the figures, it struck her that initially she must have misinterpreted the drawing. The woman wasn't holding the monster's hand; instead, there was a gap of a couple of inches between them. The monster seemed to be moving away. Even this crude a representation gave the illusion of movement.

When she switched off the lights, she resisted the temptation to stare back into the darkness of the room. There was nothing stirring in there. It was just an empty room in an old house where someone had died.

Driving back to the hotel in the dark, she began to crave company. David had not called or texted her today, but that didn't mean he wasn't thinking about her. More than once, she had used his desperation to her advantage, and before she arrived at the hotel, she knew she was going to do it again.

Sitting in the car park, surrounded by sodium lights, she sent him a text: "I'm at a hotel if you'd like to join me for a drink", and attached the Google Maps reference so he'd know exactly where to find her.

David responded immediately, as if he'd been sitting waiting for her to ask.

Back in her room, she showered and changed into a skirt and a tight black top. It was an outfit in which she felt strong and powerful; and one that she knew showed off her best features. It had been a long time since she'd seduced a man, but David was easy pickings. She didn't even feel guilty about the fact that she was going to use him for sex. It was his own fault for making himself so available.

The corridor outside her room was quiet and empty, without even background noise from any of the other rooms on that level. She stepped into the lift and pressed the button for the ground floor, checking herself out in the mirrored walls. The multiple reflections provoked a sense of loneliness. It felt strange being in the lift alone yet surrounded by herself.

When the lift doors opened, she headed straight for the hotel bar and ordered a gin and tonic from the frighteningly young-looking barman. She took her drink to a table by the window and waited. She knew that David wouldn't be long. His predictability was part of the reason she toyed with him.

Soon after, he sauntered into the bar, wearing a suit jacket and faded jeans. His look was so middle-aged it made her feel old by association. When he saw her, he raised a hand in greeting. He was all smiles. Always. The smile was a nice one; it made him seem so much more handsome than he really was.

"Jill! Hi!" He was genuinely pleased to see her.

She smiled back at him, tipped her glass. "Good to see you, David." She stood as he approached the table and leaned across it in an awkward embrace. He smelled of sandalwood and whisky, the aromas she most associated with her father. Inhaling deeply, she held on a beat too long.

"How've you been?" he sat down at the table, steepling his fingers. "I mean, how's it been, visiting the old house? Are you okay?"

Nodding, she glanced over his shoulder, checking out how busy the bar was. "It's been fine. Well, mostly."

"Would you like another drink?"

"That's a stupid question."

He stood, reached down and squeezed her hand, and turned towards the bar. He didn't even need to ask what she was drinking. He already knew. He always knew; made it his business to know. Her favoured drink, the kind of chocolates she liked, her favourite flowers. He knew it all, without ever having to ask twice, and that's why she sometimes liked having him around.

There was something different about him. Things had obviously changed since his divorce, and she was forced to admit that it suited him. He looked trimmer, and his personality had been dialled back a couple of degrees. He no longer exuded need.

She thought about this again much later, as she lay next to him in the narrow hotel bed. She watched him sleep and wondered if there had ever been any real feelings for David on her part. He was good company, an interesting conversationalist, and always put her needs first – even in bed; *especially* in bed – but anything she might have felt for him was manufactured to the point that she could no longer tell the difference between reality and play-acting.

To her, he had always been the idea of a man rather than an actual man: a presence she could conjure whenever she needed him, a male-shaped entity that never let her down.

If he had let her down even once, then maybe she'd have softened and begun to have genuine feelings towards him. Wasn't it the flaws in people that drew us towards them?

Perhaps now, all that would change. Now that he didn't view her as a potential escape route from a shitty, loveless marriage, maybe they could create something genuine.

It was late. Her emotions were all over the place.

On the wall at the other side of the room, beyond the bottom of the bed, something moved: a shadow caused by passing headlights. It took on a vague shape and reminded her of the drawing on the wall at her mother's house. If she wanted, she might have imagined clawed hands formed of shadow creeping across the wall, or the shape of a spike-topped head with a gaping mouth. But she didn't want to see those things;

she wanted to see nothing more than a simple shadow on a blank wall.

She turned onto her side, facing David. His bare shoulders looked pale in the dimness of the room. The stubble on his cheek was another layer of shadow. She reached out a hand and stroked his face; he stirred and murmured in his sleep. She wished that she could see him as a real person. She wished a lot of things, but none of them were within her power to summon and make real.

"David."

His eyes flickered open. Even the sound of her voice saying his name could pull him back into the world.

"When I was a girl, I used to draw things."

"Yeah...mmm...okay." He turned, leaning on his elbow. His eyes were sleepy, but he was almost fully awake.

"My parents never got on, and deep down I knew this. I realised that I was the glue binding them together. So I drew things for them – nice things, pretty things – in the hope that my drawings would make their world a better place. All the bad stuff, the stuff I didn't understand, got pushed down inside."

"Why are you telling me this?" His eyes were dark; they turned to black as more shadows shifted inside the room.

"I...I don't know. It's just that...I think...I think some of that bad stuff has pushed its way to the surface. Maybe my mother's death acted as a catalyst. I'm not sure. All I know is, there's something in that house that wasn't there before, an essence, a sense of despair, that has manifested in a strange way."

David shook his head. "I'm not quite sure that I understand."

She smiled. "I'm sorry I woke you."

"Never be sorry. I'm here for you. Always."

"Thank you. Go back to sleep. In the morning, I'll take you to the house and show you what I mean." She leaned over and kissed his mouth. He smiled.

That night there were no dreams. Her sleep was dark and deep and without substance. Nothing moved in the darkness; nothing stepped out to take her by the hand and lead her away.

By daylight, things were less intense. While David took a shower, she checked her phone for messages and made coffee using the little kettle on the tray by the window.

"It's all yours," said David, as he emerged from the cramped bathroom, rubbing himself down with a towel.

"You've been working out."

"A little. Since my divorce, I've been filling my time with things that make me feel happy. Being fit is one of them." He flexed his biceps, grinning.

Standing beneath the rainfall shower head, she thought about the last time she and David had met, and how he'd changed in that time. Back then, he was still married, and desperate to have her. The desperation was still there, only muted, or at least kept under the surface. She liked him better this way. It made the relationship – whatever that was – seem more mutual than before, as if they had an equal share in what was going on between them.

When she left the bathroom, David was sitting on the bed drinking coffee. He seemed relaxed; his manner was calm and reassuring. This was new. Something else of which she approved.

"What was it you wanted to show me? At the house."

She recalled last night's sleepy conversation,

and how she'd opened herself up to him, if only partially. "Let me get dressed and we can go."

He nodded. Smiled. Finished his coffee.

They used David's car. Jill felt more comfortable with somebody else driving. She had not consumed that much alcohol last night – only three or four rounds – but her head felt heavy and there was the suggestion of a headache that might form later.

"Tell me about these drawings." David kept both hands on the wheel. He'd always been a safe driver. He didn't look at her when he spoke; just kept his eyes on the road ahead.

"Drawing. Singular. It's on the wall in my mother's living room. The kind of thing I used to sketch as a kid, only...not. It's different. Darker. I never drew anything like that, not back then."

They pulled up outside the house. David got out first, going around to open the passenger door for her. An old-fashioned gesture, but one that made her feel safe.

He hung back and allowed her to take the lead, following her along the path to the front door. She fumbled with the key, and when the door opened, she had a sudden urge to step back, to turn away; but David's body was positioned so close behind her that it made such a hasty retreat impossible without barging into him.

The house had not changed overnight. She wasn't sure why she'd expected it to. The hallway was the same, the staircase was the same... everything was the same.

"This way," she said, not looking back. "In here. Tell me what you think."

She led him into the living room, switching on the light because it was so dim in there. Turning to the wall that featured the drawing, she paused for a moment, knowing that something was not right but unable to understand exactly what it was.

"Shit."

"What's up?" David stood next to her, staring at the wall.

"This isn't how it was yesterday."

The floor beneath the drawing was clear; yesterday she'd tidied away the torn pieces of wallpaper, bagged them up, and put the bag in the outside bin.

But the drawing itself had altered.

Now, instead of the family holding hands, and the mother holding hands with the monster, a gap had appeared. A space, between the little girl and the woman. So now, instead of one set of figures, there were two: the man and the little girl, and the woman and the monster.

It seemed to Jill, as she stood there looking, the drawing now depicted a mother being led – or pulled – away from a father and daughter. She was being separated – forcibly, because now that the dynamic had changed, her terrified expression made perfect sense. The woman – the mother – was afraid, yes, but she was also showing signs of hysteria because she didn't want to be taken away from her family.

"This isn't how it was... it's not the same."

"I'd say this is cute, but it isn't. In fact, it's pretty fucking disturbing." He moved closer towards her, so that they were touching. "You say you drew this when you were a kid?"

"No," she snapped, not meaning to, but getting angry at the whole situation. "That's the problem. I didn't draw it. Not this." Without thinking about it, she grabbed his hand; he squeezed her fingers, reassuringly.

"I don't understand." His voice was soft now, almost a whisper.

"Neither do I."

She let go of his hand and stepped closer to the wall, the drawing. She reached out but didn't touch it. "At the end of her life, my mother was a wreck. She barely knew who I was. I think she'd entered a fantasy world. She kept asking for my dad, and when I told her he'd died years ago, she refused to believe it. She said he was hiding from her."

Jill side-stepped in front of the drawing, examining the monster – feeling brave because David was here.

"She told me my real mother been taken from us, many years ago, and that she wasn't who we thought she was. She said she was an imposter, and now the memories she'd stolen from my real mother were being stripped away... mentally, she was gone. Her mind was broken."

"I know," said David. "I know it was tough for you, but you got through it. "This drawing... it means nothing. You're reading too much into it. This thing isn't a metaphor for your mother's mental collapse before she died. She had dementia. It tore her mind to pieces, like it does with anyone who suffers from it. You're seeing patterns that aren't there."

He thought he was being the Voice of Reason

and she knew it came from a good place, but his words were doing nothing but wind her up even tighter.

"Don't fucking patronise me, David. Just don't. You weren't there. You don't know."

He backed off; she could hear his feet shuffling on the carpet. "I'm sorry. I'm just trying to help."

Turning to him, she tried to smile. "I know, and I do appreciate it. Really. Just... just don't, okay?"

He nodded, afraid to say anything more.

Jill turned back to face the drawing. The space between the two sets of figures was wider. It had only widened by an inch or two, but it *had* widened. She was certain of it.

David drove them back to the hotel. They didn't say much on the way; the silence between them was far from a comfortable one. She didn't enjoy making him feel this way, but nor could she bring herself to try and fix the damage. She wanted to sit in silence and think about what she had seen, or felt, or both.

Was she imagining this? It was certainly possible. She might have indeed made the drawing when she was very young, as a response to the deterioration of her parents' marriage. The gap she had seen appear between the girl and the mother might have been there all along, and when she'd uncovered the image she hadn't noticed – or, more realistically, she simply hadn't acknowledged it, and had seen what she wanted to see, what she'd always wanted to see: a happy family, standing together to resist the forces of darkness.

At some point over the last couple of days, Jill realised, she had slipped into an alternative reality, a world where the animosity between her parents had been the iceberg-tip of something stranger and more horrifying; a place where a drawing on a wall could be symbolic of a darkness that had existed somewhere inside her family all along, without her even realising it was there.

"How about a drink?" said David, as he unbuckled his seatbelt. "I know I could do with one."

She stared through the windscreen, waiting for the world to reform and take on the shape it had been before. "I think that's a fucking good idea."

They went into the hotel bar and David

ordered double gin and tonics. It was good gin, expensive stuff that tasted wonderful.

They sat down at a table in the window. Outside, it began to lightly rain.

"All my life I've had an idea of the shape of things," said Jill, looking out at the drizzle. "But that idea was all wrong. The shape I had in mind wasn't the shape other people saw. My parents hated each other, and I've only just realised. God knows what went on behind closed doors in that house, when I was too young to see the signs."

David touched her hand, rubbed it gently with his thumb. "Or maybe you did know. Maybe you always knew. That's why you drew the picture, and then forgot about it."

"I don't know... I don't know anything anymore." She took another sip of gin and tonic. "When my mother died, I was glad. She'd was an awful bitch – never had a good word to say about anyone. I loved my dad. I loved him so much. When he died, nothing was ever the same again. But when my mother died, it barely made a ripple on the surface."

David was still rubbing her hand. It was nice. She drew comfort from his touch.

"Nothing in life goes to plan. All we can do is

react when stuff does happen. That's it. Control is an illusion." His voice was soft, familiar.

She laughed, but it felt strange, like a diverted scream. "I do believe you might be right. Now, let's drink up and get another one in. After a few more of these, you can take me to bed and do whatever you like."

David picked up his glass and finished his drink in one swallow. "Now you're talking." He went to the bar.

The rain intensified. By the time David returned to the table with a couple more drinks, it had reverted to that sullen drizzle from moments before. The weather, much like Jill, didn't seem to know what it wanted to do.

Several hours and too many gins later, they retired to Jill's room and fumbled around on the bed for a while. They were both too drunk and exhausted to do much more than wrestle, so it ended with them snoozing in a tangle of limbs on top of the covers.

Later, Jill woke in the dark, with a sense of dread building inside her. David was snoring. His arm lay across her chest; his legs were draped across her knees. Squirming, she extricated herself and got off the bed, staggering slightly as she made her way to the bathroom. She shut the bathroom door so that she wouldn't disturb David, and then switched on the light. In the sudden harsh glare, she saw a vague suggestion of the drawing of the monster on the wall, but the image only lasted a second or two – long enough for her eyes to grow accustomed to the bright light.

She stared at herself in the mirror. "Sober up, girl. You're freaking yourself out."

She used the toilet and washed her hands, then switched off the light. Opening the door slowly and quietly, she went back into the room. David had shifted position; he was now lying on his back with his arms outstretched. Above him, on the wall, a figure bent low, reaching with long arms to where he was sprawled on the mattress.

Jill stopped moving. She stared at the figure. It was all blackness. Unmoving. Frozen in action. Then, this image too faded and all she saw was a vague shadow on the wall. When she shut the bathroom door with her foot, the shadow dissipated.

It's got out, she thought. *Somehow, it's got out of the house.*

But surely this was nonsense, nothing but the

workings of her tired, confused mind and the effects of last night's excessive intake of gin.

Movement caught her eye: something flitting across the wall to her left. When she turned, there was nothing there. The darkness seemed to grow and swell, filling the room. She no longer felt safe here; the room was teeming with something more than the dark.

Without thinking, she grabbed her clothes from the floor and got dressed, being careful not to wake David. She had to do this alone, even if she didn't quite understand what exactly she was going to do.

Just before she left, Jill stood in the open doorway and looked back at David. The wall above the bed was empty of shadow. Nothing else moved inside the room. Reality had reasserted itself, if only for the moment.

Downstairs, she ignored the night staff as she passed the reception desk and hurried outside to her car. The drizzle had stopped but the air still felt damp. She started the car and waited, wondering if this was such a good idea after all. What if she went back to her mother's house and found the drawing had vanished? Or what if it had somehow detached itself from the wall and was waiting for her, ready to satiate an unspeakable hunger?

"Stop it," she whispered. "This isn't a fucking horror movie."

She pulled out of the parking space and drove out onto the road. Traffic was minimal, and she hit every light when it was green. Within ten minutes, she was parked outside her mother's house, sober and afraid and wishing she was somewhere else; any place far from here.

She could see from the kerb that the front door was open. Getting out of the car, she looked up and down the empty street. Nothing stirred, not even litter in the gutter. The air was still; rain threatened to return.

She approached the door and pushed it open. Walked along the hallway and into the living room. She hesitated only a moment before switching on the light.

The drawing had changed. The father and the daughter were holding hands and smiling, and the mother was nothing but a crumpled heap at their feet. Her clothing was shredded; bright splashes of red surrounded her, like the plucked petals of a flower.

The monster was no longer part of the scene.

"It's out," she said.

Then she remembered David, sleeping on the bed. That shadow poised above him, waiting for her to leave.

Jill fumbled her phone from out of her jeans pocket, almost dropping it in her haste to enter her pass code. She thumbed the phone icon and accessed David's number.

Pressing the phone hard against her ear, she wished for him to answer. The ring-tone sounded for what seemed like hours but was only seconds, and then, abruptly, it cut off. The phone went dead, not even going to voicemail. Had someone reached out and switched it off?

"David..."

She ran back to her car.

Halfway back to the hotel, the rain started to hammer down as if the elements were trying to prevent her from getting there. She turned the windscreen wipers to full and leaned down over the wheel, trying to get as close to the windscreen as possible to track a route through the washed-out gloom. Lights were smeared; the road looked like a river, and she followed it in fear of drowning.

Once she reached the hotel, she pulled up

directly outside the reception and sprinted inside. The reception desk was unmanned; the woman on night shift must have been called away. It didn't matter. Nobody could help her now; they wouldn't believe her if she tried to tell them.

Rather than wait for the lift, she climbed the stairs to the fourth floor, panting, gasping for breath by the time she reached the door of her room.

For a terrifying moment, she thought she'd lost her key fob, but then her fingers fell upon it at the bottom of her handbag, and she dragged it out and slid it into the slot below the door handle. The light turned green. She pushed open the door.

The room was dark, but not dark enough that she could not see. The bedclothes were strewn across the floor, and the bed itself was empty.

David was not there.

She walked forward, trying to convince herself that he was hiding.

"Please... David. I'm sorry. I'm sorry you were never enough for me. But you are now. I want you now. I *need* you."

She could hear nothing but a passing

motorbike on the road that ran past the hotel. Distant sirens. The soft pitter-patter of rain against the windows.

"David..."

But David was gone.

He had been taken.

Frantically, she opened the wardrobe door and dragged out the cardboard boxes she'd taken from her mother's house. She scattered the papers, not caring where they ended up, or if they were damaged. The sketch books went the same way; throwing them across the room, as far from her as they would go, she focused instead upon what else she knew was in the box, right at the bottom.

Finally, she found it: a small box of crayons.

She fumbled open the box, dropping most of the crayons on the floor; picking them up, she walked back to the bed, stood on it. Acting on instinct now – or at least some long-hidden creative impulse that had resurfaced to guide her hand, she tried to channel the repressed memories from her childhood. All the ignored signs of her mother's creeping dementia: the closed doors and hushed, yet angry voices; the nights spent trying to hear what was being said on the other side of the wall in her parents' room; the slow destruction of the idea of a happy home; the silent breakfasts; that one morning when her father had failed to hide the scratches on his cheek with her mother's cheap foundation; the following night when her father had told her that the only thing keeping him there was love for his daughter.

All of it. Each vague, hurtful scrap that she could dredge up from the pit of her memory. If she could retrieve it all from the darkness, then perhaps there was also a chance she could get to David. Reach out and drag him back from wherever he'd been taken.

Shaking, sweating, and with no idea of what she was doing or if it would even work, she started to sketch on the wall with the same blunt crayons she'd used as a child.

Right through the night. To the early hours. Crayon marks all over the hotel room walls. Her fingers rubbed down till they bled.

She was still there when they found her late the following morning, scribbling on the walls and babbling, weeping, calling out his name. Still trying to draw the monster.

Open House

They sat in the car with the engine running, staring at the house. The estate was quiet. Street lights illuminated the road and the houses in a flattering aspect; shadows pooled like black liquid in the gutters and at the bases of the pretty little trees dotted around the clusters of neat little homes.

"Well, are you going to turn it off?" Sheila glanced at the car dashboard.

"Yeah," said Bruce, turning the key to kill the engine. "What do you think?"

"My initial impressions?" Sheila looked at him, smiling in the dimness. "It has kerb appeal. Looks like a nice place. Quiet street. Good neighbourhood. Close to the shops – there's a Tesco Express around the corner – and that pub on the next street looks nice."

"That's what I thought." He glanced at his watch. "It's two minutes to. Shall we go?"

Sheila nodded. "Okay." She opened the passenger door, letting in a slight chill, and got out of the car.

Bruce looked again at the house. It was a late-nineties new-build, attractive enough, he supposed. He didn't mind it, but he doubted that he could ever love a house that was so new. Bruce had always liked old things. The house they lived in now was a Victorian terrace. The rooms were big and draughty; the yard was small but private. He loved the way it felt so old, as if the generations of lives that had passed through the house had left a mark.

He got out of the car, locked the door, and joined Sheila on the footpath.

They approached the house and Sheila knocked on the front door. She always took the lead in situations like this one. It was a natural thing; she simply pushed herself forward while he always hung back, deferring to his wife, who was five years older than him. If he ever examined the dynamic of their relationship, it was to think that he probably just liked a quiet life and let her get on with things because it was easier than engaging in some kind of psychological tug-of-war match. He supposed some people might call him hen-pecked – if that term was even still used – but he didn't care what they thought.

After something approaching half a minute, the door opened. A man stood there, dim light creeping around him from behind. He was wearing a brown sweater over a creased white shirt. Blue jeans. His hair was mid-length, his face slightly rounded. "Good evening." He flashed a nervous smile. His teeth were very white.

"Hello," said Sheila. "We're here for the viewing. "I'm Sheila Dray and this is my husband Bruce." She held out a hand; the man shook it but his grip was loose, almost feminine.

"Please, do come in," he said, opening the door wider and stepping back into a narrow, attractive hallway. He seemed distracted, as if he'd been expecting someone else.

Bruce hesitated on the doorstep. "Is this a bad time?"

"No, not at all. Come inside."

They followed him into a neat kitchen. Strip lights illuminated the room but not enough to make things clear. A woman – presumably the man's wife – was standing with her back against a workbench and sipping something from a glass. Her eyes were bleary.

"Hello," said Bruce.

The woman raised her glass. "Hi. Just take your time and look around." She took a drink.

"As you can see," said the man – who still hadn't introduced himself – this is the kitchen. It isn't huge, but it's certainly big enough for entertaining guests." He smiled, laughed softly, as if he'd made a joke. "Plenty of storage space, too." He walked on, towards a double doorway. "Through here we have the dining room. A bigger space; perfect for dinner parties."

It went on like that: the man giving them the tour, laying on the soft soap, with Bruce and Sheila following behind. The house was nice but it wasn't anything special. Bruce thought that his initial reaction had been correct. He couldn't picture them living here, within these walls, moving through these newish rooms while they thought about older ones.

After they'd seen the whole house – kitchen, dining room, lounge, toilets, bedrooms – and the small, well-kept garden, the man left them alone upstairs to have a look around without suffering his scrutiny.

"So, what do you think?" Those words... they were becoming her mantra: *What do you think? How do you feel about this one?*

He shook his head. "It's... okay. I'm just not feeling it."

"Me neither. It's a nice house, but I don't think it's us."

Back downstairs, they said their farewells and left the house. Bruce glanced back over his shoulder as they walked down the drive. The lounge curtain fell quickly back into place across the main window, as if whoever was looking out at them didn't want to be seen. He was left with the impression of a small, pained white face. They got back into the car and drove away, heading for home.

That night as they lay in bed, Sheila browsed through listed properties online. She had her tablet on her knee and was using her index finger to flip through photographs that all looked the same: rooms, doorways, smart little gardens. Carbon-copy houses for modern clones.

"Do you think we'll find something?"

Sheila shrugged. "I hope so. We need more

space. If your mother is going to come and stay for a while, we need at least another bedroom, a second bathroom, and an additional reception room." She didn't look at him, just at the screen. The light washed her face pale, draining the colour from her cheeks.

Bruce closed his eyes and wished that his sister wasn't such a bitch. It always fell upon him to look after their mother, and now that she was suffering from Alzheimer's they were going to have to take her in, give her a home. She was no longer well enough to look after herself. She often forgot his name. At times, it seemed as if she were speaking to strangers.

"We have another couple of viewings this week," said Sheila, breaking into his sombre mood. "Maybe one of those will be better." She smiled, put her tablet on the bedside cabinet, leaned over and switched off the reading lamp. She didn't even say goodnight. Bruce could still remember a time when she'd kissed him on the lips each night before turning over and going to sleep. These days they slept with several inches of mattress between them. Everything changed, even old things, even things that had remained the same for so long. Nothing lasted.

"That couple. The ones at the house..." He stared at the back of her head as he spoke.

"What about them?"

He paused. "Did they seem... well, a bit odd to you?"

"They were slightly nervy, I thought." She shifted position, as if she were being careful not to touch him. "The bloke – the husband – he was as jittery as a house cat."

"They were a bit weird."

She sighed, altering her position slightly on the mattress. "It's a false situation, though, isn't it, showing a stranger around your house, letting them into your home? Some people might get nervous. It's kind of invasive."

"I suppose," he said, and turned onto his side. He listened to Sheila's breathing for a while and then closed his eyes, imagining what he might do, or how he might feel, if her breathing simply stopped.

Bruce didn't sleep well that night. Whenever he did manage to slip into a doze, his mind was plagued by images of pursuit. He was never sure who or what was chasing him, or why he was running away, but he seemed to be fleeing along identical streets of shuttered houses, past shattered street lamps, and no matter how fast he tried to move he was dogged by the feeling that something was slowly gaining on him – and it was utterly relentless; it would not stop until it had caught up with him.

~

When morning came, he felt as if he'd had no rest at all. His eyes stung; his head felt as if overnight it had been stuffed with cotton: a dull, soft pressure beneath his skull. House-hunting was causing him more stress than he'd expected. Bruce didn't like change; he preferred things to stay the same, however unreasonable that might seem.

A couple of days later they had another viewing, this one at the other end of town. The house had been built in the eighties, so it was slightly older than the last one they'd seen, but still Bruce couldn't help thinking of it as new. They were all new, these houses. They had been built over the old land and whatever history it contained. Sometimes he liked to believe that the old would rise up again and banish the new, rupturing the thin skin of modern society and bleeding through the wounds.

"What do you think?" Sheila's familiar refrain.

"It looks okay," he said. "But I don't really know this part of town."

"Me neither." She reached out and rested her hand on the plastic dashboard, her fingers twitching like small animals. She made a fist, as if to stop them moving, and then relaxed it. "Let's give it a chance, though. Time's not on our side."

They got out of the car and walked over to the house. Bruce opened the gate for Sheila and as she walked through it, and along the narrow pathway, she didn't even thank him.

This time the door was opened before they even had a chance to knock. The man who stood in the doorway was short, heavy-set, and was wearing tracksuit bottoms and a baggy t-shirt.

"Hello." Sheila smiled but took a step backwards, away from the man.

"You 'ere for the viewing?" His accent was thick and guttural; a local man, probably born and bred in the area.

"If that's okay, yes."

The man shrugged and turned away from them. Bruce half expected him to slam the door in their faces, but he didn't: he left the door open and stalked away down the hallway.

"I suppose we'd better go in."

Sheila took a hesitant step, and then another, more confident one, as she followed the man inside.

It was only as he closed the door behind him that Bruce realised what had been bothering him since he'd first laid eyes on the man: he looked the same as the man from a couple of days ago, the owner of the last house they'd viewed. Perhaps not identical – certainly not in his overall build – but he had similar features: they had the same colour eyes and shared the shape of a face. Indeed, the two men might have been brothers, or cousins. Perhaps they were indeed related. It wasn't unusual for family members to live in the same town, even in this modern era of mass movement and people following the jobs around.

"Downstairs bog," said the man, pointing at a doorway under the stairs. "We never bother using it." He twisted his mouth in what was clearly meant to be a smile and displayed teeth that were brown and uneven.

Sheila glanced inside and moved on. Bruce didn't bother looking; he just followed his wife through into the kitchen. One of the overhead spotlights was defective; it flickered in a regular tempo. The kitchen was small and cluttered, but it was at least clean.

"My missus likes to cook," said the man, answering a question that had not been asked.

"It's... very homely." Sheila's voice had raised an octave, as it always did whenever she felt uncomfortable in her surroundings.

The man trudged through another doorway, reaching out to switch on the lights. It was a living room, but one that did not seem to have seen much life. The wallpaper was out of date; there were no pictures on the walls. The carpet was threadbare but, again, it was not dirty. There was no television, no stereo, and the only furniture was a tall, empty bookshelf.

"They lead out into the garden." The man pointed at a set of French doors. Beyond them, the overgrown garden seemed to press up against the glass, dark fingers of shrubbery trying to reach inside and grab them.

"Lovely, I'm sure." Sheila moved closer to Bruce. He could sense her discomfort.

"Upstairs," said the man, as if it were a command.

As they turned to leave the room, Bruce

caught sight of a framed photograph lying face down on one of the bookcase shelves. The man had left the room, expecting them to follow. Bruce reached out and turned the photograph over, standing it upright. It depicted the man and a woman who must surely have been his wife. They stood in a large, empty field, leaning against each other. The woman, he noticed, looked a lot like the wife in the last house they'd seen. Her features were disarmingly similar, despite the differences in her body shape, and her hair was much darker – so dark in fact that it looked as if it were dyed.

"Come on... let's get this over with. I don't like this one." Sheila jabbed him in the side with her elbow and walked ahead of him out of the room. Slowly, he followed, wishing that he'd not seen the photograph. He wasn't quite sure why, but it had unnerved him. He felt as if he'd seen something he shouldn't have: an atrocity, a thing that should not be witnessed.

Upstairs the house was just as basic as it was on the ground floor. Only the kitchen, it seemed, showed signs of habitation. Bruce imagined these people – the man and his absent wife – living only in that single room, eating at the table, sleeping beneath it, standing around drinking coffee and looking out of the windows, longing to be allowed outside.

It was growing dark when they left the house, hurrying out of the gate, across the road, and to the car.

"Bloody hell... that was a bit odd." Sheila's eyes were huge, her cheeks were taut.

"There was a strange feeling in that house, wasn't there?" He unlocked the car and opened the passenger door for his wife.

"It felt like a serial-killer's lair," she said. "Like a place where someone has been killed, or where somebody might be killed in the future." She slid into the passenger seat and pulled the door shut, locking out the evening. "*Brrrrr*," she said, theatrically, hugging herself as if she were freezing.

Bruce walked around the car and slid behind the wheel. He glanced back at the house and it looked vacant, as if nobody lived there, or had ever lived there. The lights were off. He could barely remember having been inside the house: even the memory of the vendor was fading, as if he'd been just a dream. Bruce started the engine and pulled away from the kerb, desperate for the warmth and solace of his own home, where nothing had ever changed, and everything was safe and old and belonged to him.

~

The following day at work was a quiet one. He sat behind his desk and pretended to revise spreadsheets and check lists of items that had gone out of the company's main warehouse for delivery. Nobody called him on the phone and the few emails he received were vague and non-committal, promises of future orders or hints that bills might be paid soon.

Bruce struggled to summon any interest in what he was doing. He'd worked at the depot for fifteen years now and his time there became less and less memorable as the years spun by, each one blending into the last and the next, forming a long, smudged sense of a working life rather than a real one.

Perhaps the house move – if they ever found one they liked – would stir things up a little, refresh what had become so stale. He had the feeling that Sheila was hoping for this, but for his own part he wasn't even sure if he cared anymore. He was going through the motions, doing what he felt he was meant to do, and hoping that something would happen to force his hand. If he was honest, he was faking it, but he had been doing so for so long now that it had stopped feeling like an act and become the truth. Other people's expectations defined how he lived his life – his wife, his mother, even the people he worked with.

How had he reached this point? These people, the ones he shared the world with, meant less to him every day. His mother was slipping so far away from him that he no longer recognised her; his wife was a pale imitation of the woman she'd once been, a ghost, a shred torn off something more substantial.

Bruce left work early, knowing in his heart that nobody would even notice his absence. He drove aimlessly for a while through streets which grew grubby and unwelcoming and parked the car on a quiet alley behind a row of boarded-up shops.

He watched as a stray dog urinated up against a wall decorated with abstract spills and splashes of graffiti. The dog scratched at its hind quarters, its thin legs twitching. After a minute or so it trotted slowly away.

Hands shaking, Bruce turned up the volume on the stereo, waited until the song reached its crescendo, and then he began to scream. But the scream echoed only inside his head, mute yet deafening; it never emerged into the real world.

He drove home, emptying his mind of all thought, trying to achieve some level of peace by simply thinking of nothing. Somewhere at the back of his mind, a void shivered.

Sheila was waiting for him when he arrived home.

"This is the last viewing we have in our diary. If it's no good... well, I don't know what we'll do." Her face was drawn; she looked exhausted. For a moment he felt like reaching out and drawing her close to him, hugging her as hard and as tightly as he could. But the moment passed: inaction caused his emotions to fizzle out like a dying ember.

"Just let me get changed and we can be off. It'll only take a minute."

She sat down on the sofa with her hands in her lap, knees pressed tightly together, eyes staring at the empty face of the television.

~

They pulled up outside the house a minute later than their appointment. It was on a slightly run-down street in a less-than-desirable area. Not too shabby, but enough that it was never really a serious consideration, just a sketchy back-up option.

Bruce switched off the engine and turned to his wife. "We could always just go. Turn around and leave."

She frowned. "Why would we do that? We need to find somewhere."

"I...I don't want to move. Don't want to change. I can feel things shifting and it isn't comfortable. I'm afraid of what might happen next."

The muscles in Sheila's cheeks twitched, and then relaxed. "What are you talking about?"

"I don't know. It just doesn't feel right."

"This isn't really the time to be discussing it. Let's just go inside and have a look and we can go from there. We might hate it. We might love it. I don't know. This is all out of our hands... your mother..." She looked down, at her hands, her knees. "Why did this have to happen? Everything was so... so nice and dull. I don't want this kind of excitement."

He reached out and clasped her hand,

tightening his fingers around her palm. There was no response: she didn't even look up. Her skin was cold.

"Come on" he said, letting her go.

The front door was scarred and faded. This part of town was less exclusive than anywhere else they'd looked, but things were getting desperate. They'd reached the end of their list. There was nowhere to go after this.

The house was old, at least: a battered Victorian terrace, but much bigger than the one they currently owned. It stood tall and imposing, set back from the road at the end of a long front garden with a paved drive. Weeds stood up through the gaps in the paving. The bins were overflowing.

The door opened before Sheila had raised a hand to knock. The man on the threshold looked withered. That was the only word Bruce could think of to describe him.

"Come," he said, stepping back inside the house. Behind him, the light was dim and yellowish, like swamp gas.

Sheila stepped inside, leaving Bruce no choice but to follow her. The hallway was bare. No carpets, no wallpaper, nothing on the walls.

Even the skirting boards had been stripped. He recalled that the estate agent had called the place a "doer-upper", stating that it needed work. He had not lied.

"Follow," said the man up ahead of them, whose form seemed to diminish the deeper into the house they went.

He'd looked like the other men who had shown them around the last two houses. Not identical, but at least similar enough to have some kind of racial resemblance. Like a distant ancestor, or perhaps a primitive version of the same subspecies.

There were no bulbs in the light fittings, no lamps to be seen inside the house, and Bruce could not detect the source of the sickly yellow light that seemed to fill the place with its dim presence yet offered little by way of actual illumination.

Empty rooms without doors gaped on either side of the hallway. Bruce thought of open mouths and hungry beasts, of things waiting to be fed. Those rooms were empty in a way that seemed to define the word. There was nothing inside them, not even air; and yet still he sensed that strange insatiable hunger.

"Hurry," said a voice up ahead, presumably

urging them on because its owner realised this house would be of little interest to them and he wanted to get the viewing process finished as quickly as possible. His single-word exclamations were beginning to irritate Bruce. It was as if the man couldn't even be bothered to put together a coherent sentence.

They were reaching the end of the hall, where the light was weakest and the shadows gathered like a thick dust against the walls and the floors. A door opened ahead of them; it was nothing more than a black oblong in the wall. Bruce faltered, not wanting to enter, but Sheila kept going, seemingly oblivious of the increasingly strange nature of the situation in which they found themselves.

"Wait... just a minute..." But his words were lost; she either didn't hear him or chose to ignore his call. He watched with a vague sense of unease as she vanished into the darkness of the open doorway.

Bruce didn't want to follow his wife inside, but he had no choice. He never did. He'd followed her for their entire married life; she had always been the leader and he a willing disciple, hanging on her coattails.

So he stepped through the open doorway,

wondering only distantly what had happened to the odd man who'd been showing them around. The puppet-like man who was merely a small part of what was happening here, much like the people they'd met in the other houses. Each of them parts of the same whole; appendages of whatever waited for them here, in the dark.

The door whispered shut behind him. He couldn't see a thing, just the slow, rhythmic pulsing of the darkness around him.

This, he thought, *must be what's it's like to float in outer space.*

"Sheila?"

Slightly ahead of him, but close enough to make out clearly, he heard a whimper.

"Please, Sheila... talk to me..."

She whimpered again. He knew it was her. It could not have been anyone else. It was a sound he was not used to hearing: his wife breaking down and submitting to defeat.

"What's happening?"

"*Welcome,*" said a voice that sounded cobbled together from other voices: a sound that was somehow less than the sum of its parts, an exclamation that formed words by accident rather than design. It was almost an anti-voice, not meant for communication at all. A noise, just a noise in all that swirling darkness...

Sheila whimpered again, and then stopped abruptly, as if the sound had been cut off in mid-exhalation. Then he heard a wet, soft gurgling and the collapsing weight of something heavy as it slumped to the floor.

Close to breaking, Bruce reflected that this was not a property viewing in the traditional sense. They had not been looking at these houses; the houses had been inspecting them. And now, at last, they had been chosen.

"*Welcome*," the voice said again.

Even before the yellow light came on and he met the owner of that voice, he knew what he would see: a further descendant of the homeowners he'd met previously, a cruder, more rudimentary rendition of the figures who had guided him through the old rooms of their new homes. The ancient, formless face of his and Sheila's new landlord.

"*Welcome home*," said the strangled composite voice.

Then the light flickered, briefly lighting up the room and what it contained, and Bruce began to scream.

Story
Notes

Text Found on a Defunct Website was first published online, under a different title. It's a mere ditty; a short, sharp shock, inspired by examining countless Estate Agent websites. Nothing more – and possibly a lot less – than that.

The Chair was inspired by the sight of a dining chair left abandoned one night outside a house on my street. It's my attempt to examine the loneliness caused by parental abandonment and the failure of the family unit. Physically absent father. Mentally absent mother. Placebo medication and mental health. Old houses and abandoned furniture.

With **The Table**, I wanted to take a further look at the main character from "The Chair", but years later, when he was an adult, and focus on the way his trauma was still with him, and how it left him open to… other influences. The past as an enemy. A domestic situation turned sour. Domestic furniture as a doorway to the supernatural.

I'm not quite sure what prompted **On the Walls**. It started life as a shorter piece called "The Cabinet" and is the final part of Ben's story (even though he doesn't appear in it). I wanted to see what happened to his girlfriend, Jill. She was a loose end that needed tying. As I wrote the story, it changed completely and became a story about childhood, broken families, and mental collapse. The cabinet vanished and was replaced by a drawing on a wall. A lot of my recent life experiences bled into its creation. There's a fair bit of pain between this story's lines.

Open House was inspired by the tedious experience of my wife and I viewing houses when we decided to buy a bigger place. You meet some odd people during this process. We moved into our current (forever?) house three years ago, but during the search my mind started working on scenarios where the people conducting the viewings looked the same, and each subsequent house became dimmer, grimmer, and less welcoming than the last.

I'd like to thank Andy Cox, Gary Fry, and, of course, Steve Shaw, for helping these stories into the world. And into your homes.

Also by Gary McMahon:

Novels
Late Runners (Angry Robot, 2005)
Rain Dogs (Humdrumming, 2008)
Hungry Hearts (Abaddon Books, 2009)
Pretty Little Dead Things (Angry Robot, 2010)
Dead Bad Things (Angry Robot, 2011)
The Concrete Grove (Solaris, 2011)
Silent Voices (Solaris, 2012)
Beyond Here Lies Nothing (Solaris, 2012)
The Bones of You (Earthling Publications, 2013)
The End (NewCon Press, 2014)

Collections
Tiny Torments (ZedHed Press, 2003)
Dirty Prayers (Gray Friar Press, 2007)
How to Make Monsters (Morrigan Books, 2008)
Different Skins (Screaming Dreams, 2009)
Pieces of Midnight (Ash-Tree Press, 2010)
Tales of the Weak & the Wounded (Dark Regions Press, 2012)
Where You Live (Crystal Lake Publishing, 2013)

Novellas & Chapbooks
Breaking Hearts (D-Press, 2004)

Rough Cut (Pendragon Press, 2006)
All Your Gods Are Dead (Humdrumming, 2007)
The Harm (TTA Press, 2010)
What They Hear in the Dark (Spectral Press, 2011)
Thin Men with Yellow Faces (with Simon Bestwick) (This is Horror, 2012)
Nightsiders (DarkFuse, 2013)
Reaping the Dark (DarkFuse, 2014)
The Night Just Got Darker (KnightWatch Press, 2015)
The Grieving Stones (Horrific Tales Publishing, 2016)

Visit Gary McMahon at his website:
garymcmahon.com

Now available and forthcoming from
Black Shuck Shadows:

blackshuckbooks.co.uk/shadows

Printed in Poland
by Amazon Fulfillment
Poland Sp. z o.o., Wrocław